Making Room

By Phoebe Koehler

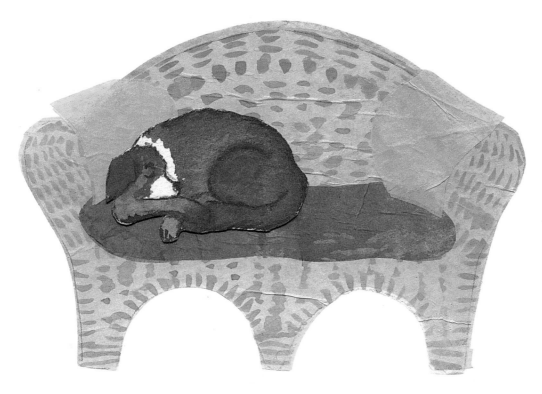

BRADBURY PRESS ·· NEW YORK

Maxwell Macmillan Canada · Toronto
Maxwell Macmillan International
New York · Oxford · Singapore · Sydney

The illustrations were done in tissue and construction paper collage
using hand colored papers.
The pictures were color-separated by scanner and reproduced in four colors using
red, blue, yellow, and black inks.

Bradbury Press
Macmillan Publishing Company
866 Third Avenue
New York, NY 10022

Maxwell Macmillan Canada, Inc.
1200 Eglinton Avenue East
Suite 200
Don Mills, Ontario M3C 3N1

Macmillan Publishing Company is part of the Maxwell Communication Group of Companies.

First edition
Printed and bound in the United States of America
10 9 8 7 6 5 4 3 2 1
The text of this book is set in Clearface Bold.
Typography by Julie Y. Quan

Library of Congress Cataloging-in-Publication Data

Koehler, Phoebe.
Making room / written and illustrated by Phoebe Koehler. — 1st
American ed.
p.   cm.
Summary: Happily living alone with his master, a likable mutt's life
changes when his master's household expands to include a new wife,
cat, and baby.
ISBN 0-02-750875-7
[1. Dogs — Fiction.]   I. Title.
PZ7.K817725Mak   1993
[E] — dc20   91-41356

To Lotte's good master
Tom

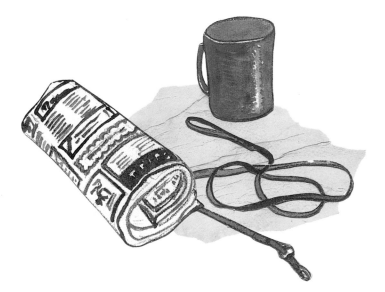

i am the dog of a
good master.

We share everything:
long walks at sunrise,

lazy lunches in the kitchen,

cozy evenings on the couch.

Or did until that lady came along.

Now my master is in
such a hurry I get
just one tiny block
in the morning.

They eat out all the
time. When they come
home they forget to
bring a doggie bag.

And I have to
lie on the floor.

But—
she plays a
great game
of chase,

whips up the finest dishes for me to clean,

and scratches me
behind the ears
just right.

Or did until that cat came along.

Now the cat hides
all my best toys
under the couch.

I'm forced to
share every dish
in the kitchen.

I'm lucky to get
a quick pat on the
head.

But–
this cat puts up a great fight,

shares his milk
(sometimes),

and helps keep the bed warm.

Or did until that baby came along.

Now we have to
tiptoe about
the house.

There's never enough milk to go around.

And we both have
to sleep on the rug.

But–
we take long walks again.

I find
wonderful
tidbits on
the floor.

And the baby makes me laugh.

So I guess I'll make room.